This Little Tiger book belongs to:

_____

_____

_____

Here Comes the

by Kathryn White Illustrated by Michael Terry

Crocodile

LiTTLE TiGER

LONDON

It was hot in the deep green jungle when Crocodile leapt from the river. He sniffed and snarled, growled and snapped. The jungle shook and quivered. His long tail whipped as he scuttled along. "I want food to make me strOOOng."

Brown Monkey came
swinging down, to Crocodile's
hungry delight. Crocodile snatched
poor Monkey's tail and Monkey
screeched in fright.

"Oh Crocodile don't you eat me or your
sharp teeth will wobble and drop. You'll go skinny
and sag like a crocodile bag and your great jaws will
dribble and flop. I'm made of sickly chocolate,"
Monkey chattered with glee.

"I knew that," said Crocodile,
creeping away. "You're too
small a snack for me."

Crocodile felt hungrier than ever when he spied through his big beady eyes, two flamingos dancing together: "Now here's a tasty surprise." Crocodile sneaked through the water with a hungry glint in his eye. "Two treats I see, as pink as can be, I'll snatch them before they fly."

The flamingos chuckled and fluffed, "Why, don't even take one lick. We're both made of strawberry candy and are bound to make you quite sick. You'd howl and you'd yowl and you'd grimace. You'd swell and you'd tumble and roll." "I knew that," said Crocodile, lying, "I've only come out for a stroll."

Crocodile marched off defeated with a gurgling
hole in his tummy. He spotted an elephant drinking:
"Elephant dinner, yummy." Into the water he slithered
as swift as a snake in the grass.
And when he got to where Elephant was . . .
he leapt up as quick as a flash.

"Oh Crocodile don't you
eat me or your jaws will
jangle and lock.
It's quite clear to see you
can't eat me for tea because
I am made of rock."
"I knew that," said Crocodile
blushing. "You're a boulder
as big as can be. I'm just out
for a walk, no time to talk
as I'm meeting
a dear friend for tea."

Then Crocodile spied a zebra, grazing lazily
out on the plain. Crocodile's tummy rumbled,
gurgled, and grumbled, hungry for food again.
Crocodile crept through the grass as silent
as he could be.
"I'll sneak up behind him quickly and gobble
up Zebra for tea."

"Oh Crocodile, don't you
eat me or you'll turn spotty
and pink from dark green.
You'll splutter and sneeze
and have wobbly knees,"
said Zebra, polite and serene.
"But you're only a zebra,"
said Crocodile. "You're only
a bright, stripy horse."
"But my black stripes are very
hot pepper and my white
stripes are salt, of course."

"Oh boo hoo!" yowled Crocodile, shedding big tears. "I feel like I haven't eaten in years." He blubbered and bawled and wallowed and squalled. He rolled on his back, which looked very funny, then wailed, "I just want some food in my tummy!"

"Don't worry," said kindly young Zebra, "you can share all my grass with me." The two pink flamingos brought treats to share, with Monkey's bananas for tea. "And I've brought some clear, cool water," said Elephant, squirting a spray. And Crocodile grinned with his big sharp teeth and said, "What a wonderful day!"

It was hot in the deep green jungle
as the animals played by a tree, when
Tiger leapt out from behind them,
growling, "I am ready for tea!"

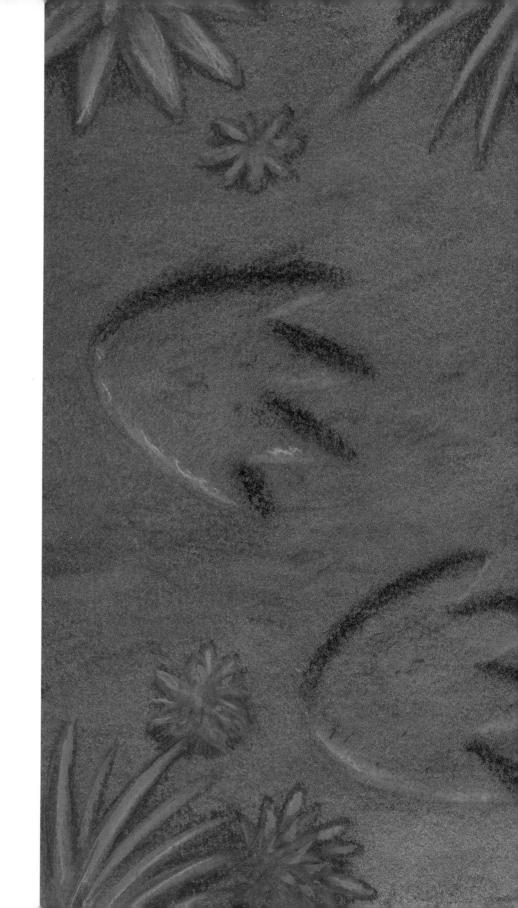

For Charlie, my inspiration
~ K. W.

To my son, Jamie,
my little crocodile
~ M. T.

LITTLE TIGER PRESS LTD,
an imprint of the Little Tiger Group
1 Coda Studios, 189 Munster Road, London SW6 6AW
www.littletiger.co.uk

First published in Great Britain 2004
This edition published 2018

ISBN 978-1-84869-799-7

Printed in China • LTP/1800/2262/0418
2 4 6 8 10 9 7 5 3